HORTON HEARS A WHO!

By Dr. Seuss

RANDOM HOUSE • NEW YORK

TM & copyright © by Dr. Seuss Enterprises, L.P. 1954, copyright renewed 1982.
All rights reserved.
Published in the United States by Random House Children's Books,
a division of Random House, Inc., New York.

RANDOM HOUSE and colophon are registered trademarks of Random House, Inc.

www.randomhouse.com/kids
www.seussville.com

Educators and librarians, for a variety of teaching tools, visit us at www.randomhouse.com/teachers

Library of Congress Cataloging-in-Publication Data
Geisel, Theodor Seuss, 1904–1991   Horton hears a Who!   By Dr. Seuss [pseud.]
New York, Random House [1954].
unpaged   illus.   29 cm.
I. Title.   PZ8.3.G276Ho   54-7012
ISBN: 978-0-394-80078-3 (trade) — ISBN: 978-0-394-90078-0 (lib. bdg.)

Printed in the United States of America   107

For My Great Friend,
Mitsugi Nakamura
of Kyoto,
Japan.

On the fifteenth of May, in the Jungle of Nool,
In the heat of the day, in the cool of the pool,
He was splashing . . . enjoying the jungle's great joys . . .
When Horton the elephant heard a small noise.

So Horton stopped splashing. He looked toward the sound.
"That's funny," thought Horton. "There's no one around."
Then he heard it again! Just a very faint yelp
As if some tiny person were calling for help.
"I'll help you," said Horton. "But *who* are you? *Where?*"
He looked and he looked. He could see nothing there
But a small speck of dust blowing past through the air.

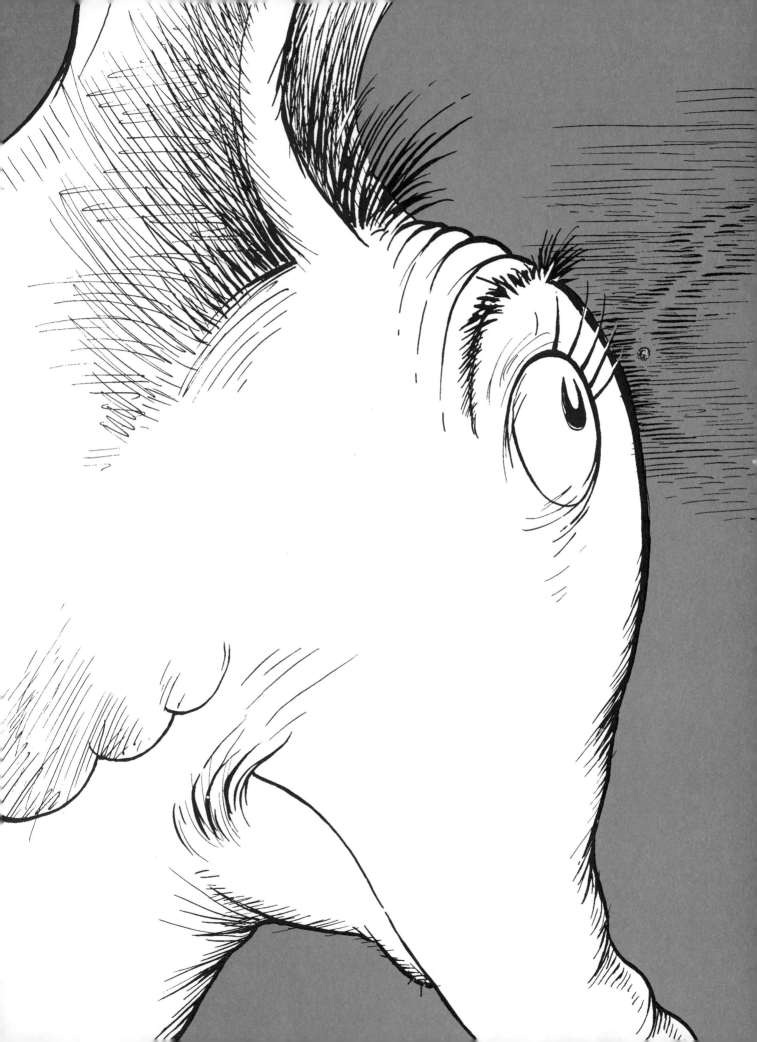

"I say!" murmured Horton. "I've never heard tell
Of a small speck of dust that is able to yell.
So you know what I think? . . . Why, I think that there must
Be someone on top of that small speck of dust!
Some sort of a creature of *very* small size,
Too small to be seen by an elephant's eyes . . .

". . . some poor little person who's shaking with fear
That he'll blow in the pool! He has no way to steer!
I'll just have to save him. Because, after all,
A person's a person, no matter how small."

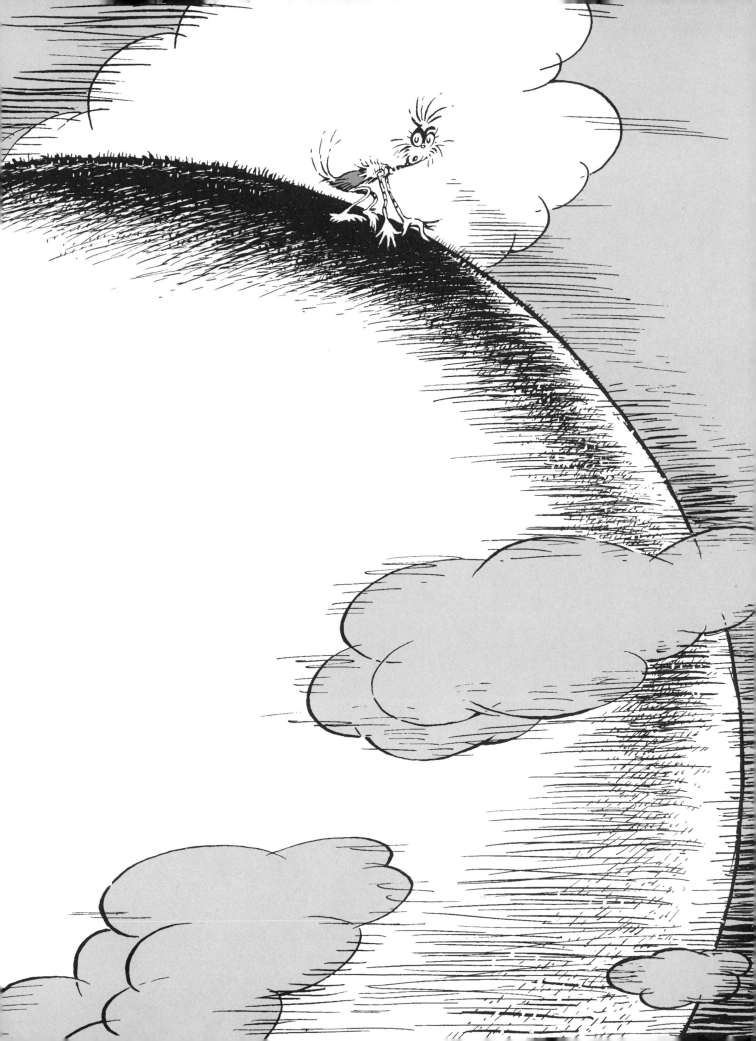

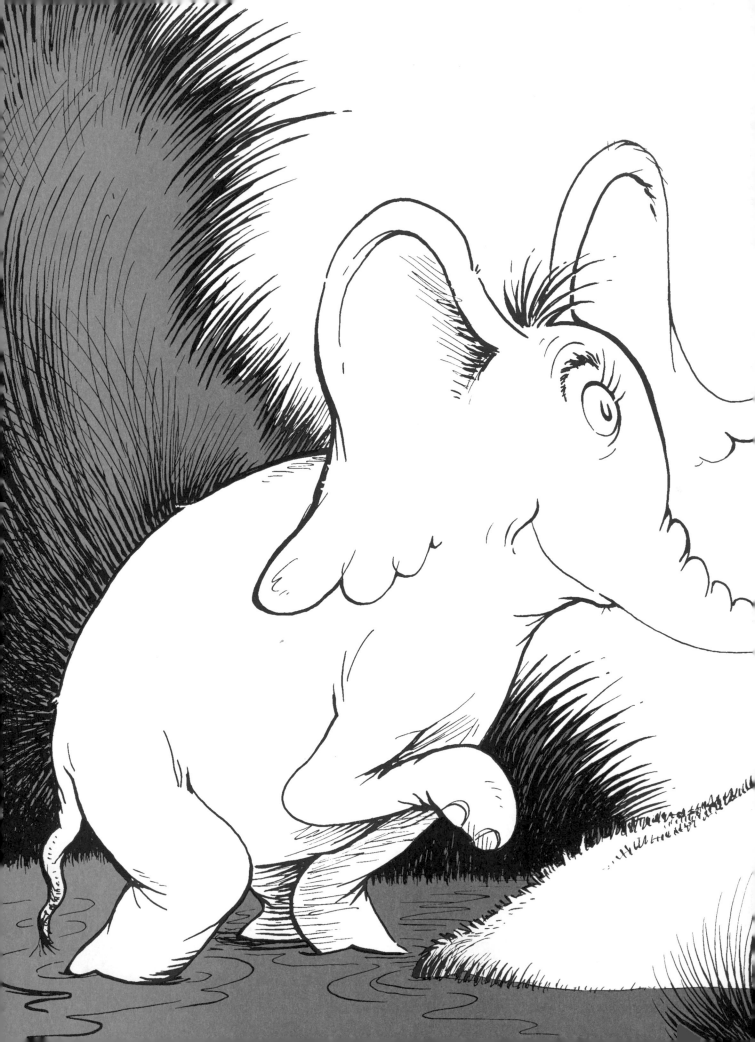

So, gently, and using the greatest of care,
The elephant stretched his great trunk through the air,
And he lifted the dust speck and carried it over
And placed it down, safe, on a very soft clover.

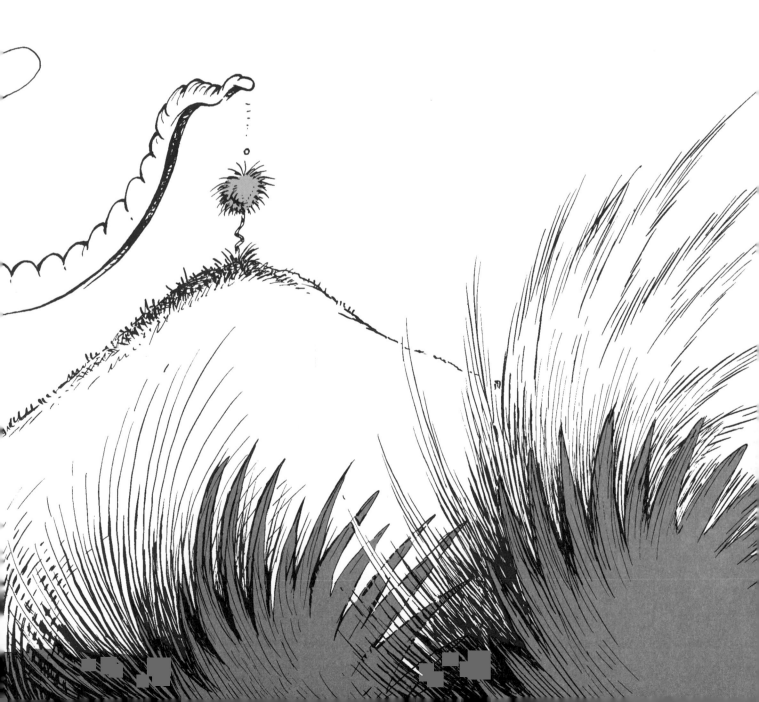

"Humpf!" humpfed a voice. 'Twas a sour kangaroo.
And the young kangaroo in her pouch said "Humpf!" too.
"Why, that speck is as small as the head of a pin.
A person on *that?* . . . Why, there never has been!"

"Believe me," said Horton. "I tell you sincerely,
My ears are quite keen and I heard him quite clearly.
I *know* there's a person down there. And, what's more,
Quite likely there's two. Even three. Even four.
Quite likely . . .

". . . a family, for all that we know!
A family with children just starting to grow.
So, please," Horton said, "as a favor to me,
Try not to disturb them. Just please let them be."

"I think you're a fool!" laughed the sour kangaroo
And the young kangaroo in her pouch said, "Me, too!
You're the biggest blame fool in the Jungle of Nool!"
And the kangaroos plunged in the cool of the pool.
"What terrible splashing!" the elephant frowned.
"I can't let my very small persons get drowned!
I've *got* to protect them. I'm bigger than they."
So he plucked up the clover and hustled away.

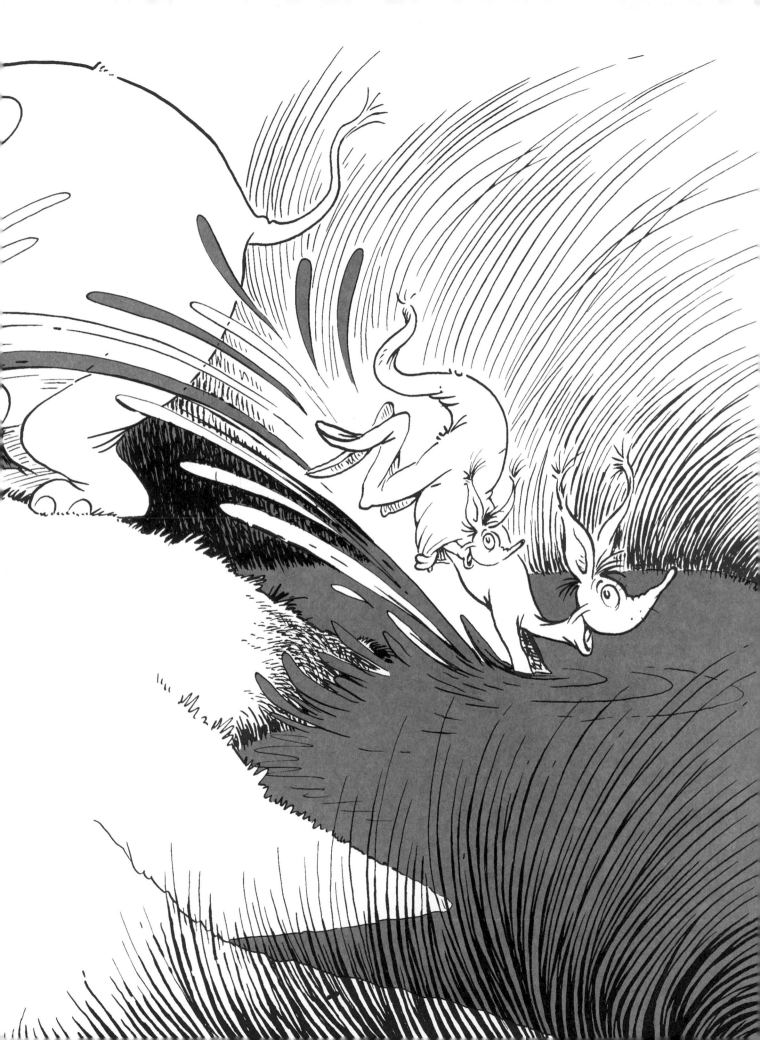

Through the high jungle tree tops, the news quickly spread:
"He talks to a dust speck! He's out of his head!
Just look at him walk with that speck on that flower!"
And Horton walked, worrying, almost an hour.
"Should I put this speck down? . . ." Horton thought with alarm.
"If I do, these small persons may come to great harm.
I *can't* put it down. And I *won't!* After all
A person's a person. No matter how small."

Then Horton stopped walking.

The speck-voice was talking!

The voice was so faint he could just barely hear it.

"Speak *up,* please," said Horton. He put his ear near it.

"My friend," came the voice, "you're a *very* fine friend.
You've helped all us folks on this dust speck no end.
You've saved all our houses, our ceilings and floors.
You've saved all our churches and grocery stores."

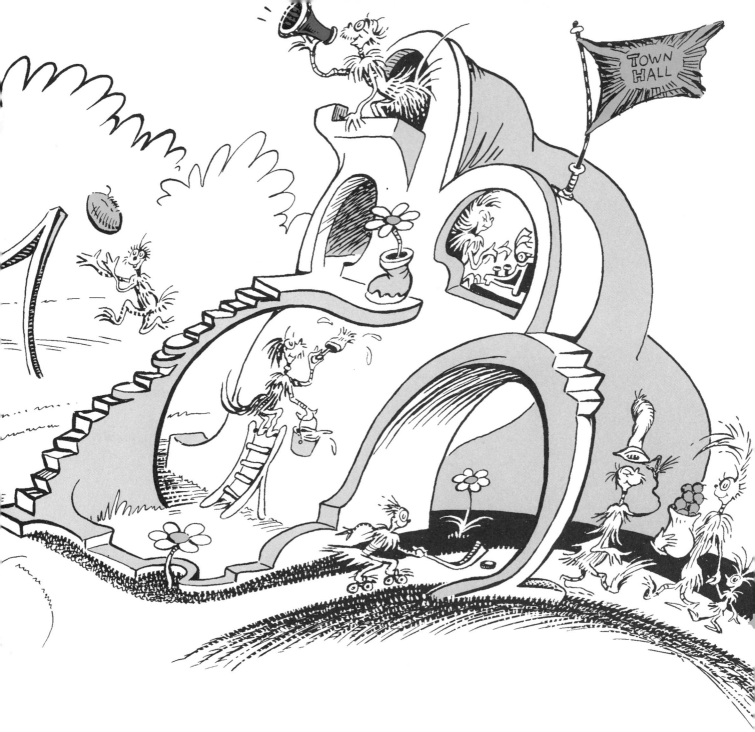

"You mean . . ." Horton gasped, "you have *buildings* there, *too?*"
"Oh, yes," piped the voice. "We most certainly do. . . .
"I know," called the voice, "I'm too small to be seen
But I'm Mayor of a town that is friendly and clean.
Our buildings, to you, would seem terribly small
But to us, who aren't big, they are wonderfully tall.
My town is called *Who*-ville, for I am a *Who*
And we *Whos* are all thankful and grateful to you."

And Horton called back to the Mayor of the town,
"You're safe now. Don't worry. I won't let you down."

But, just as he spoke to the Mayor of the speck,
Three big jungle monkeys climbed up Horton's neck!
The Wickersham Brothers came shouting, "What rot!
This elephant's talking to *Whos* who are *not!*
There *aren't* any *Whos!* And they *don't* have a Mayor!
And *we're* going to stop all this nonsense! *So there!*"

They snatched Horton's clover! They carried it off
To a black-bottomed eagle named Vlad Vlad-i-koff,
A mighty strong eagle, of very swift wing,
And they said, "Will you kindly get rid of this thing?"
And, before the poor elephant even could speak,
That eagle flew off with the flower in his beak.

All that late afternoon and far into the night
That black-bottomed bird flapped his wings in fast flight,
While Horton chased after, with groans, over stones
That tattered his toenails and battered his bones,
And begged, "Please don't harm all my little folks, who
Have as much right to live as us bigger folks do!"

But far, far beyond him, that eagle kept flapping
And over his shoulder called back, "Quit your yapping.
I'll fly the night through. I'm a bird. I don't mind it.
And I'll hide this, tomorrow, where *you'll* never find it!"

And at 6:56 the next morning he did it.
It sure was a terrible place that he hid it.
He let that small clover drop somewhere inside
Of a great patch of clovers a hundred miles wide!
"Find THAT!" sneered the bird. "But I think you will fail."
And he left
With a flip
Of his black-bottomed tail.

"I'll find it!" cried Horton. "I'll find it or bust!
I SHALL find my friends on my small speck of dust!"
And clover, by clover, by clover with care
He picked up and searched them, and called, "Are you there?"
But clover, by clover, by clover he found
That the one that he sought for was just not around.
And by noon poor old Horton, more dead than alive,
Had picked, searched, and piled up, nine thousand and five.

Then, on through the afternoon, hour after hour . . .
Till he found them at last! On the three millionth flower!
"My friends!" cried the elephant. "Tell me! Do tell!
Are you safe? Are you sound? Are you whole? Are you well?"

From down on the speck came the voice of the Mayor:

"We've *really* had trouble! Much more than our share.
When that black-bottomed birdie let go and we dropped,
We landed so hard that our clocks have all stopped.
Our tea-pots are broken. Our rocking-chairs smashed.
And our bicycle tires all blew up when we crashed.
So, Horton, *please!*" pleaded that voice of the Mayor's,
"Will you stick by us *Whos* while we're making repairs?"

"Of course," Horton answered. "Of course I will stick.
I'll stick by you small folks through thin and through thick!"

"Humpf!"
Humpfed a voice!
"For almost two days you've run wild and insisted
On chatting with persons who've never existed.
Such carryings-on in our peaceable jungle!
We've had quite enough of your bellowing bungle!
And I'm here to state," snapped the big kangaroo,
"That your silly nonsensical game is all through!"
And the young kangaroo in her pouch said, "Me, too!"

"With the help of the Wickersham Brothers and dozens
Of Wickersham Uncles and Wickersham Cousins
And Wickersham In-Laws, whose help I've engaged,
You're going to be roped! And you're going to be caged!
And, as for your dust speck . . . *hah! That* we shall boil
In a hot steaming kettle of Beezle-Nut oil!"

"*Boil* it? . . ." gasped Horton!
"Oh, that you *can't* do!
It's all full of persons!
They'll *prove* it to you!"

"Mr. Mayor! Mr. Mayor!" Horton called. "Mr. Mayor!
You've *got* to prove now that you really are there!
So call a big meeting. Get everyone out.
Make every *Who* holler! Make every *Who* shout!
Make every *Who* scream! If you don't, every *Who*
Is going to end up in a Beezle-Nut stew!"

And, down on the dust speck, the scared little Mayor
Quick called a big meeting in *Who*-ville Town Square.
And his people cried loudly. They cried out in fear:
"We are here! We are here! We are here! We are here!"

The elephant smiled: "That was clear as a bell.
You kangaroos surely heard *that* very well."
"All I heard," snapped the big kangaroo, "was the breeze,
And the faint sound of wind through the far-distant trees.
I heard no small voices. And you didn't either."
And the young kangaroo in her pouch said, "Me, neither."

"Grab him!" they shouted. "And cage the big dope!
Lasso his stomach with ten miles of rope!
Tie the knots tight so he'll *never* shake loose!
Then dunk that dumb speck in the Beezle-Nut juice!"

Horton fought back with great vigor and vim
But the Wickersham gang was too many for him.
They beat him! They mauled him! They started to haul
Him into his cage! But he managed to call
To the Mayor: "Don't give up! I believe in you all!
A person's a person, no matter how small!
And you very small persons will *not* have to die
If you make yourselves heard! *So come on, now, and TRY!*"

The Mayor grabbed a tom-tom. He started to smack it.
And, all over *Who*-ville, they whooped up a racket.
They rattled tin kettles! They beat on brass pans,
On garbage pail tops and old cranberry cans!
They blew on bazookas and blasted great toots
On clarinets, oom-pahs and boom-pahs and flutes!

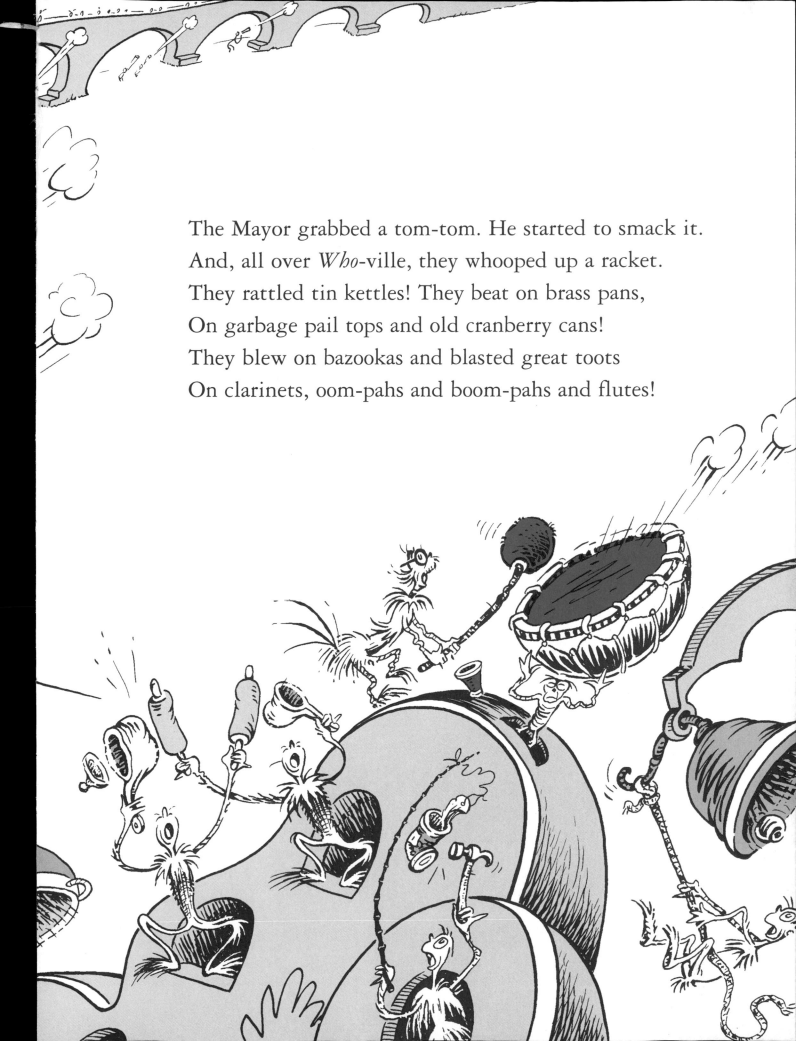

Great gusts of loud racket rang high through the air.
They rattled and shook the whole sky! And the Mayor
Called up through the howling mad hullabaloo:
"Hey, Horton! *How's this?* Is our sound coming through?"

And Horton called back, "I can hear you just fine.
But the kangaroos' ears aren't as strong, quite, as mine.
They don't hear a thing! Are you *sure* all your boys
Are doing their best? Are they ALL making noise?
Are you sure every *Who* down in *Who*-ville is working?
Quick! Look through your town! Is there anyone shirking?"

Through the town rushed the Mayor, from the east to the west.

But *every*one seemed to be doing his best.

*Every*one seemed to be yapping or yipping!

*Every*one seemed to be beeping or bipping!

But it *wasn't enough,* all this ruckus and roar!

He HAD to find someone to help him make more.

He raced through each building! He searched floor-to-floor!

And, just as he felt he was getting nowhere,
And almost about to give up in despair,
He suddenly burst through a door and that Mayor
Discovered one shirker! Quite hidden away
In the Fairfax Apartments (Apartment 12-J)
A very small, *very* small shirker named Jo-Jo
Was standing, just standing, and bouncing a Yo-Yo!
Not making a sound! Not a yipp! Not a chirp!
And the Mayor rushed inside and he grabbed the young twerp!

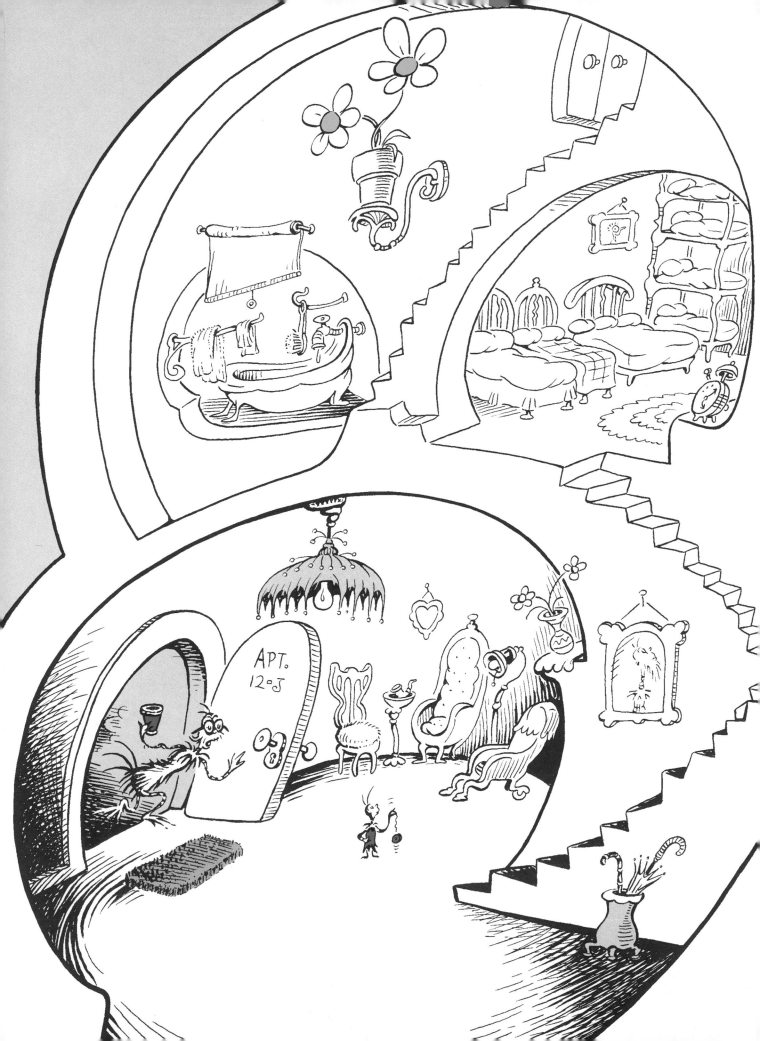

APT.
12-J

And he climbed with the lad up the Eiffelberg Tower.
"This," cried the Mayor, "is your town's darkest hour!
The time for all *Whos* who have blood that is red
To come to the aid of their country!" he said.
"We've GOT to make noises in greater amounts!
So, open your mouth, lad! For every voice counts!"

Thus he spoke as he climbed. When they got to the top,
The lad cleared his throat and he shouted out, "YOPP!"

And that Yopp . . .

That one small, extra Yopp put it over!

Finally, at last! From that speck on that clover

Their voices were heard! They rang out clear and clean.

And the elephant smiled. "Do you see what I mean? . . .

They've proved they ARE persons, no matter how small.

And their whole world was saved by the Smallest of All!"

"How true! Yes, how true," said the big kangaroo.

"And, from now on, you know what I'm planning to do? . . .

From now on, I'm going to protect them with you!"

And the young kangaroo in her pouch said, . . .

". . . ME, TOO!
From sun in the summer. From rain when it's fall-ish,
I'm going to protect them. No matter how small-ish!"